When Santa Claus receives Christmas letters from children, he becomes very busy preparing for Christmas Eve. That is the busiest night of all for Santa, as this simple story shows.
Can Santa deliver all the presents before children everywhere wake up on Christmas morning?

Available in Series S846 Square format Bible Stories
The First Christmas

LADYBIRD BOOKS, INC.
Lewiston, Maine 04240 U.S.A.
© LADYBIRD BOOKS LTD MCMLXXXV
Loughborough, Leicestershire, England
Printed in England

Santa Claus
has a busy night

written by LYNNE BRADBURY
illustrated by JON DAVIS

Ladybird Books

At the North Pole, Santa Claus had been busy for weeks. He had received hundreds of letters from boys and girls, all telling him what presents they wanted for Christmas.

He had sorted out the letters
and made a long, long list…

dolls
bikes
puzzles
books
clothes
boats
planes
paints
watches
radios
computers
trains
games
skates
pencils
balloons

And then, on the other side, he had
written the children's names and
where they lived so that he would
know where to go.

At last it was Christmas Eve, the night before
Christmas. Santa Claus had been even busier
that day, filling his sacks and loading them
onto his sleigh.

He fed his reindeer and got them ready to pull the heavy load. Rudolph, with his bright red nose, was at the front to lead the others.

Then Santa went to get ready.

First he put on
his red trousers.

Then he put on
his red coat.

Next he put on
his red hat.

And last, he put on
his big black boots.

Soon all the children would be going to bed.

Santa hoped that they would all be asleep by the time he arrived.

He had so many places to visit.
It was time to go...

Santa Claus drove his sleigh up, up into the sky!
Through the clouds and back down over
sleeping towns and cities.

Down, down to the rooftops,
where Santa stopped his sleigh.

Then Santa took one of his heavy sacks and climbed down the first chimney.

He filled the children's stockings with presents from his sacks. Every time Santa left a present, he checked a name off his list.

Some people left Santa cookies or a piece of cake. He was very pleased. Climbing up and down chimneys made him hungry!

Being Santa Claus wasn't an easy job. There were houses where the chimneys were too small and houses with no chimneys at all.

Some children were sick and in the hospital, and others were staying at a different house. But Santa didn't forget anyone.

He climbed hundreds of stairs and tiptoed in and out of dark rooms to leave his presents.

And all the time, Rudolph and the other reindeer pulled the sleigh from place to place.

Santa Claus went to places that were cold and snowy. Brrr!

He went to places that were wet and
windy—and once he nearly lost his hat!

He flew over high mountains...

...sandy deserts

...and the oceans.

On and on through the night sky flew
Santa Claus...

He even went to hot countries where it was
summer and not winter.

Phew! In those places Santa wished he could take off his thick red coat and his big furry boots. Christmas was going to be a very hot day for the children there!

Finally Santa Claus put a check next to the last name on his list. He had finished. All the sacks were empty!

It would be daylight soon, and children everywhere would be waking up.
"Time to go home, Rudolph!" he said.

When Santa got back to the North Pole, he fed his tired reindeer and put them to bed.

Then he went into his house, took off his hat, his coat, and his boots, and sat in his big chair by the fire.

Now it was Christmas Day.

Santa Claus thought about all the places he'd visited. By now the children would be awake. He hoped they liked their presents.

Some children hadn't been given *all* the things they'd asked for—Santa just couldn't carry any more. Some children would remember to say thank you, and others would forget. Oh, well!

After his busy night, Santa Claus went to sleep. But there's one thing we've forgotten in this story—

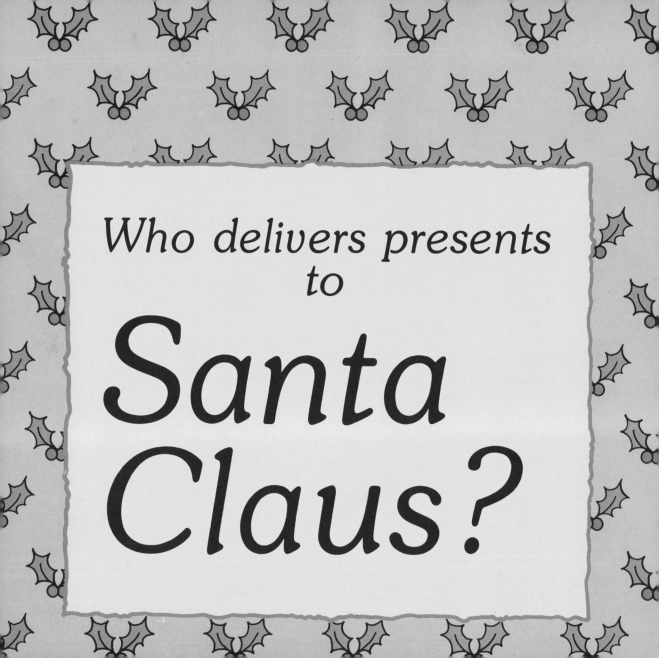

Who delivers presents
to
Santa
Claus?